Mommy's Having a Watermelon

Mommy's Having a Watermelon

by Danny and Kim Adlerman

illustrated by Megan Halsey

The kids at Our House

The Kids at Our House
47 Stoneham Place
Metuchen, NJ 08840

www.dannyandkim.com
info@dannyandkim.com

Library of Congress Cataloging-in-Publication Data available on request

ISBN-10: 0-9705773-9-7 (hc)   ISBN-13: 978-09705773-9-9 (hc)
ISBN-10: 0-9705773-0-5 (sc)   ISBN-13: 978-09705773-0-6 (sc)

Printed in China
10 9 8 7 6 5 4 3 2 1(hc)   10 9 8 7 6 5 4 3 2 1 (sc)

The display type was set in Jazz.
The text type was set in Caslon 224 Book.
Manufactured in China
Book production and design by *The Kids at Our House*

Danny and Kim make school and library appearances. In fact, we also appear in front of big people—at conferences, county reading councils, professional development workshops...we can fit into most any venue you can think of! For more information, as well as free activities and activity guides, check out www.dannyandkim.com.

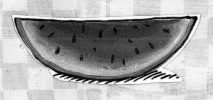

Contents

For Kevin, Stephanie, and Carlos

—K.A. and D.A.

For Jodi & Sonya—who gave birth to two of my
favorite babies, Lil and Zak

—M. H.

Chapter 1

The Picnic

Mommy is having a watermelon.

I know it's crazy, but it's true.

She's having a watermelon, and it's all my fault!

It all started early last summer.

We were having a picnic behind our house—Mommy, Madeleine, Mrs. Hanes and me. I'm Zoe Rind.

Madeleine and I had so much fun telling stories and jokes.

I laughed and laughed until my drink came out of my nose!

We had lunch at the picnic table near the big oak tree.

We ate peanut butter and jelly sandwiches and sipped lemonade.

That's when it happened.

We munched on watermelon while we
fooled around and laughed.

A seed flew out of my mouth and
landed—

Ping!—right in Mommy's glass.

Mommy wasn't paying attention.

She picked up her glass and swallowed her lemonade down in one big gulp.

Madeleine and I laughed even harder.

We laughed so hard I fell off the picnic bench.

"My, you two certainly have the giggles," Mommy said.

"What's so funny?" Madeleine's mom asked playfully.

"Oh, nothing," Madeleine started, trying to keep the laughter inside her mouth.

"Silly girls," Mrs. Hanes sighed as she started clearing the table.

We stopped giggling. I caught my breath.

Then I remembered something my older brother, Richie, said a long time ago.

He told me not to swallow seeds

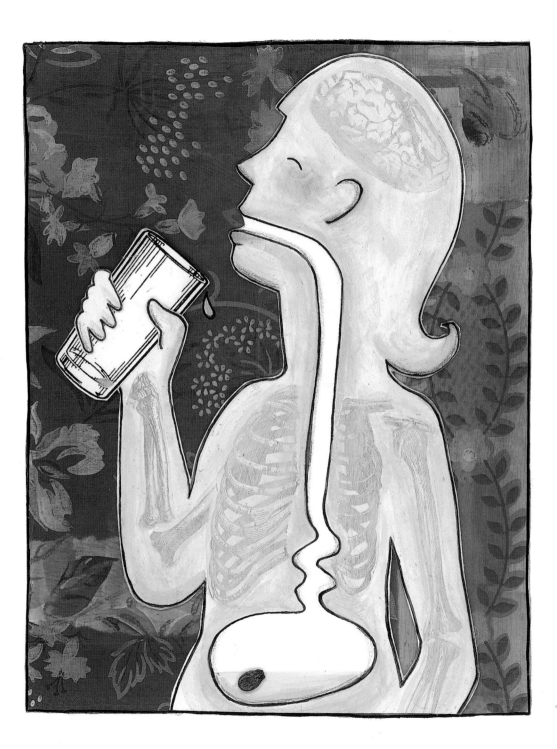

and pits, or else they would grow in my stomach.

That's when I started to worry....

Chapter 2

Mommy Doesn't Feel Well

But soon I forgot all about that picnic.

And I forgot all about what Richie said…until a month later when Mommy complained that she hadn't been feeling well.

Mom was tired, and sometimes she had a tummy ache.

Once Daddy said to her, "It must have been something you ate."

He turned to Richie and winked.

That's when it hit me.

If it was something she ate, it was *definitely* my fault.

But in the fall, Mommy complained less about feeling bad.

She stopped running to the
bathroom so much and started to eat
a lot.
    I started to feel better myself.
    Until the day after Thanksgiving....

Chapter 3

Run for Help

Richie came into the kitchen and patted Mom's stomach.

"You look like you've got a watermelon in there!" he said.

I almost choked on my leftover turkey.

"Could I go to Madeleine's house for a little while?" I squeaked.

I did *not* feel like being in that kitchen with Richie, Mommy and her watermelon anymore.

MOMMY BELLY X-RAY MACHINE

"Sure, Zoe, but don't be too long,"
Mommy told me.

I ran out the kitchen door straight to
Madeleine's house.

I didn't stop until I reached her room
and closed her bedroom door.

"What's wrong?" Madeleine asked.

I took a deep breath and blurted,

"Maddy, I am in trouble. Mommy is
having a watermelon and it's my fault
and it happened when I spit that seed
into her glass which was an accident
and we laughed and laughed and now I
feel awful and you can't tell anyone and
you have to promise and I don't know
what to do....

Madeleine's eyes widened. "Are you sure?" she asked.

I nodded.

"Wow. A watermelon. That's big, all right," she said.

"What should I do?" I asked. Madeleine usually had good advice.

"First you have to make absolutely sure that it's a watermelon," she said thoughtfully. "Then you should apologize."

I thought about the time I gave our dog a haircut.

Mommy forgave me then.

I remembered the time I broke Richie's model airplane.

He forgave me too.

Talking to Madeleine made me feel a little better.

Maybe, just maybe, if I confessed, my parents would forgive me again.

I marched home knowing what I had to do.

I had to make sure about the watermelon.

Then I would beg for forgiveness.

Chapter 4

The Big Talk

When I got there, my parents were sitting in the living room.

"What made you so big, Mommy?" I asked, startling them both.

"Well," Mom answered, "there's a special seed inside me growing, and it makes me grow too. When it finishes growing, and it's ready, it will come out."

A seed. Growing. They knew exactly what it was.

"But what is it?" I asked, wanting to be extra sure.

Mommy said, "We don't know yet. We don't want to find out before it happens.

"We want to be surprised."

I was afraid they would be *very*
surprised….

"I didn't think they came from mommies,"
I said hesitantly.

Mommy replied, "Well, honey, where did
you think they came from?"

I thought about it. "The ground, I guess...."

"You mean like a cabbage patch?" Dad asked.

"Sort of," I answered. "I guess more like a melon patch, really."

Mommy grinned and told me she understood.

"Isn't it exciting?" Daddy asked, smiling.

I didn't know what was so exciting about having a watermelon.

I didn't know why they were so happy.

And I wondered what he meant when he said, "We couldn't have plant it better ourselves."

Then I realized I had an even bigger problem....

My parents were strange.

Then I started to wonder where the melon would go after it came out of Mommy.

Would it go to the fruit section at the supermarket?

Would we save it and eat it next summer?

I didn't know how I felt about that.

Chapter 5

Waiting and Worrying

It wasn't long after our talk that Daddy woke me up in the middle of the night.

"Pumpkin," he called, shaking me softly. "It's time for you and Richie to go to Grandma's."

"What's going on?" I asked, yawning and stretching.

"Mommy and I are going to the hospital now. It's going to come out soon!" he replied excitedly.

"Okay," I said as I got dressed quietly but quickly.

I went to school the next day, but I really couldn't think about anything other than the watermelon.

I thought about it all day long.

I didn't know if I wanted our melon to go to the supermarket.

And I didn't think I could eat it in the summer.

Chapter 6

A Special Delivery

Later that day, Grandma took us to the hospital and we went right upstairs.

There was Mommy, lying in bed.

A nurse came to the door wheeling a little cart.

"Special delivery, Mrs. Rind!" she called out.

She lifted a bundle out of the cart and handed it to Mommy.

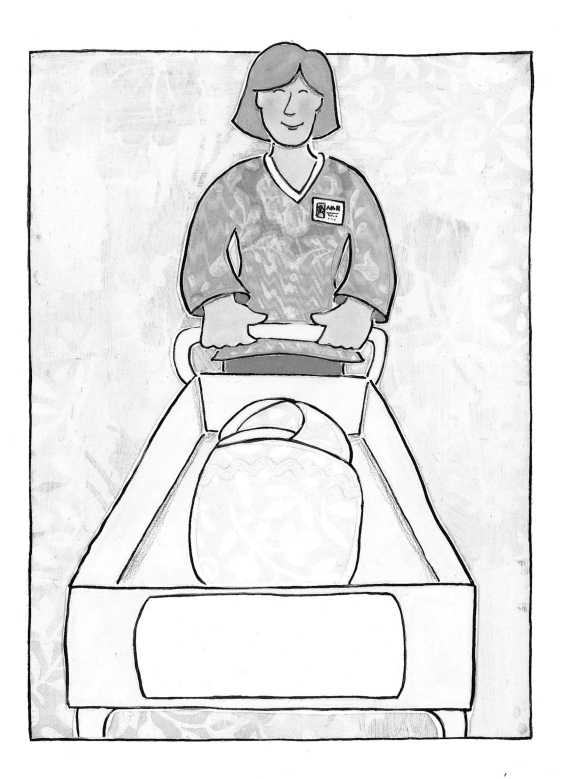

I raced over, curious to see the mysterious new watermelon.

But it wasn't a watermelon at all....

"A baby girl! A little baby girl! Mommy, you had a *baby*!" I shrieked.

"Well of course, honey, what did you think we would have?" she asked.

"Umm..." I said, turning to Daddy and smiling. "A boy."

"What are we going to call her?" Richie asked.

Daddy put his arm around me.

"Hmm...what do you think, sweetheart?"

"How about Melonie?" I said.

"Melonie Rind?" Dad, said, laughing. "I think I like it!"

I can't wait to tell her where she
came from.

Growing Tips

Do you want to grow a yummy watermelon of your own? You can, you know, almost anywhere in the United States. If you live in USDA Zone 3 or lower (mostly the northern tier of the Midwest and parts of Alaska), choose short-season melons and protect your patch from chilly temperatures. Leave the bigger melons to folks farther south. You'll have better luck with smaller ones—and since they mature early, you can enjoy them sooner!

Besides the classic red, watermelon flesh can be orange, yellow or white—these melons taste similar to those with the more traditionally colored insides. Some gardeners say the nonstandard shades are harder to grow.

You should have:

Compost Maker	Garden Hose	Mulch
Fertilizer	Garden Trowel	Shovel
Floating Row Covers	Plants or Seeds	

Step 1: Make sure your patch gets full sun and is protected from cool spring and fall winds. A south-facing slope is ideal.

Step 2: Mix plenty of organic matter into the soil to provide the conditions watermelons like: a light, sandy, fertile loam (soil mixture including clay, sand and fiber) that is well drained yet retains moisture.

Step 3: Sow seeds directly into the garden if your growing season is long enough for the plants to mature (check your seed packet). An inch deep should do it. If you have a short season, it's OK to use small plants from your local nursery. Be careful, though: Watermelons don't like to be transplanted, especially as they get older.

Step 4: Make sure your soil is ready at planting time, even if you added plenty of organic matter earlier. For each plant, dig a hole 2 feet across and 1 foot deep, and add at least a shovelful of compost or gardening manure and a trowel or two of bone meal.

Step 5: Allow lots of space between plants—from 3 feet (for small varieties) to 12 feet apart (for giant ramblers).

Step 6: Spread a thick organic mulch to stifle weeds and hold in moisture. If you use black plastic mulch with slits cut for the plants, it will hold in heat better than soil covering. Remember, though, to reuse it each year, whether on watermelons or other crops, as it is important to be environmentally responsible. Use heavy 6-mil black poly; it will have a 10- to 20-year life.

Step 7: If you can, cover your plants with floating row covers to keep the air warm. Give young plants an inch of water a week.

Step 8: Remove the covers when flowers appear— they need bees and other insects to pollinate them! If you compost, fertilize with compost tea every few weeks.

Step 9: Watermelons should be ready to pick about 35 days after your plants are in full bloom.

Watermelon Recipes

Frosted Watermelon

Ingredients

Seedless watermelon cut into 1/2- to 3/4-inch-thick slices

Yogurt

Granola or similar cereal

Instructions

Using your favorite cookie cutters, cut shapes out of watermelon slices. Or, if you prefer, use classic cut watermelon wedges. Frost with vanilla or other flavor yogurt. Sprinkle with granola.

Thanks to the National Watermelon Promotion Board for permission to use these recipes.

BLUEBERRY
DATE

CHERRY
DATE

BLACKBERRY
DATE

Watermelon Game Cube

Ingredients

25 equal-size cubes each of watermelon, white jack cheese, yellow cheddar, smoked turkey and summer sausage

1 cup ranch dressing

Instructions

Build a game-style cube by methodically alternating cubes, making a 5-cube x 5-cube layer for the base. Build four more layers on top, forming a tight cube. Serve with the ranch dressing. Serve with picks. Serves 4 to 6.

Watermelon in a Blanket

Ingredients

12 premade or purchased crepes

2 tablespoons cinnamon sugar

12 seedless watermelon "logs," each 1 inch by 8 inches, drained to remove excess moisture

Vanilla and lemon yogurt for dipping

Instructions

Sprinkle one side of the crepes with cinnamon sugar and place a watermelon log at the end of each. Roll them up and serve with the flavored yogurts for dipping. Serves 12.

Watermelon Dippers

Ingredients
- 8 ounces sour cream
- 4 tablespoons sugar
- 1 teaspoon vanilla extract
- Watermelon sticks or small wedges

Instructions
Blend together the sour cream, sugar and vanilla in a small serving bowl. Use as a dip for the watermelon.

Stir

Mix

35